Tales Around The Fire

(Ovihambarere)

Vetira Rukoro

with illustrations by Ufuomaoghene Akpokiniovo

Pan African Publishing House
Dallas, Texas, United States

Book Design: C.Nichole
Illustrations: Ufuomaoghene Akpokiniovo

Published in the United States by Pan African Publishing House under exclusive license from Vetira Rukoro.
www.PanAfricanPublishing.com

Printed in the United States of America

ISBN: 979-8-9873599-4-5

Tales Around The Fire

(Ovihambarere)

TABLE OF CONTENTS

WORDS OF WELCOME

Storytelling in many African cultures is a thread connecting generations and weaving wisdom through time. That is why I am excited to welcome you to this book, which I see as my own humble continuation of this tradition. Within these pages, you'll discover eight folklore tales from my tribe, the Namibian Ovaherero people, translated and retold in a new and refreshing way.

As children we waited for nightfall to hear these tales because, as the legend goes, anyone who told tales during the day would grow a monkey's tail. I do suspect that our parents cleverly fabricated this myth to avoid children nagging them for stories during the day. But once it was night, we gathered by the glow of the fire to hear these ancient tales retold.

Now through these pages, I invite you to claim your seat by the fire to discover the ancient wisdom of the Ovaherero people.

The Helper Boy

Once upon a time, in the African drylands there lived a tall man with his herd of cattle. He was a dark brown *Himba* man, who had a black mash of hair that he trimmed every winter's end. The man lived in a hut made of cattle manure that was topped with a grass rooftop.

Having lived alone for a very long time, he had grown accustomed to a daily routine of cattle herding and star gazing.

He rose every day before sunrise and left his hut for the same adventure. After he had sipped his morning cup of tea, he strolled towards the mooing crowd that waited patiently for him to open the cattle enclosure.

Once inside, the cattle marched straight to the water point. The man smelled the familiar odor of cattle manure as he followed them into the enclosure. There he tarried on with his only companions and spoke to them of the tales he still remembered.

When midday came, he opened the enclosure and led the cattle to lands he knew they could graze well on. He strolled behind them, swinging his shepherd's stick as they went. After he led them far enough, he turned around and headed back home. He ended his days by eating dinner, drinking another cup of tea, and, finally, watching the horizon with unwavering awe. The sinking sun glared through the branches of the Acacia trees and left the earth with an orange and red portrait that was sure to leave the

"

best artsman jealous. Then the stars opened their eyes to shine through the night's sky. One by one, the man named the stars in a slow mutter: 'Vega, Deneb, Arcturus, Polaris...' He knew them all by heart, or rather by the countless lessons his father had sat him through.

'Now son, when you get lost, follow the Polaris star and it will lead you back home. This North Star has helped many lost men find their homes again,' he remembered his father's husky voice saying.

When the man grew tired, he would retreat to his hut and go to sleep.

* * *

Summers came and went, and the once-young man aged into the now-old man. All his life he knew the changes each season promised, but this summer was different. This summer was the driest the old man had ever experienced. There were a few Acacia trees that were spread throughout the landscape, but with their short stems and thorn branches, they did very little to shade the now cracking soil.

Thin clouds formed only to tease the thirsty grounds, but were yet to spill a single drop of water. Everything stood wait for the flooding rains, and this made things harder for the old man. He had grown weaker over the years and now the old man had to lead his cattle even further to find good grazing land. Grasping his walking stick harshly, he staggered along after his herd of cattle. After some time, there was virtually no good land left for the cattle to graze on, and the cattle began to thin.

One night, after his daily routine, the old man sat by his fire in silence. He watched as the fire ate away the wood he had piled on. The fire let out small *tit* and *tat* noises as if to thank him for the wood. The only other sound the old man could hear was that of laughing hyenas and mooing cows in the distant darkness. In this wonted night, the old man looked up and began to name the stars,

'Vega, Deneb, Arcturus, Po...'

He stopped and looked around. He could not see the twinkle of the Polaris star in the sky. He rubbed his eyes and looked again, but still, nothing. *Ah, I must just be tired,* he thought. So he walked to his hut and went to sleep.

The next morning, he woke up and made himself a fresh cup of tea. When he had finished brewing his daily dose of vitamins, he silently drank his concoction. This part of the day was his favourite. The sun could not yet be felt, but from underneath the earth, it had already driven away the darkness. He breathed in the cool morning air and sighed at the beauty of it all. He was about to finish his cup of tea when he realised that the cows were more restless than usual. He hastily walked over to them, ready to kill what he figured would be a snake.

When he reached the herd, instead of a thin bag of poison, he was met with the innocent smile of a young black boy.

'Young boy, where have you come from?' the old man asked as he looked around for an answer to his question.

The boy was clothed in an old loincloth and had a beaded necklace. His hair was braided in two cornrows that affirmed his youth to the old man.

'I have come to help you with your cattle, if you will have me?' the young boy answered.

'I have no money to pay you my son,' replied the old man.

His land was isolated from the rest of the villagers, which meant that he never got visitors. He was so excited to finally have someone to talk to that he blurted out almost too quickly,

'B-bu-but food I have plenty of! I will feed you well if you stay on and help me herd my cattle.'

'Okay Uncle, I accept. However, I will take care of the cattle alone, and you are not to come with me. You are old and are to spend your time resting!' the young boy demanded.

The old man saw no need for resistance. He shook the boy's hand, and with that they started their new arrangement.

And so, the old man and the young boy began to live together. They developed a new routine. Every morning the boy woke up, made tea for the old man, and then headed towards the cattle. After the cows drank their share of water, he walked joyfully behind them as he led them to grazing fields. The old man sat at the fire and watched on feeling confident about his new helper.

At night the two would joke and laugh about tales from the old man's past. After the young boy went to sleep, the old man would look up at the stars, but he still could not find the Polaris star. It did not bother him much as he figured that with his age, he had simply forgotten where it was. When he grew tired, he went to bed.

Weeks went by and the cattle started gaining lots and lots of weight. The old man began to wonder where the boy was feeding the cattle.

He remembered that he had promised to let the boy deal with the cattle herding alone, but he couldn't help but be curious. He had been herding his cattle alone for fifty-five years and he had never seen them look this good. So he could not understand how this young boy managed to get them so fat despite the ongoing drought that surrounded them. The old man had to find out what was going on. So he made up his mind to follow the boy the next day.

When morning came, the old man watched as the young boy worked his daily routine. When he saw that the boy was making ready to lead the cows to the grazing lands, he stood up and followed in a haste.

The old man followed the humming noise the boy left behind. He followed closely behind, hugging the trees as he went. They walked on for a few more miles before the boy suddenly stopped and turned around.

★ ★ ★

The young boy was humming a song as he followed the wagging tails of the cows that were trying to beat the flies away. He decided to walk further today, feeling no rush to be back home. As he walked, the sun beamed off of his now glistening skin. The boy stopped to wipe off a drop of sweat that was trailing down his face when he heard a twig snap behind him. He quickly turned around and saw the old man avoiding his gaze.

‘I told you not to follow me old man, and you agreed! Are you not a man of your word?!’ the boy demanded.

‘I could not help myself. I am sorry, I will go back home right away,’ the old man mumbled as he retreated to their home.

At home, the young boy reminded the old man never to follow him again. He forgave him and they continued to live together.

A few days passed and the old man found himself thinking about the boy again. He could not help but wonder where the boy was taking the cattle. He knew the path the boy was taking, because he had taken it many times before, but he never ran into good grazing fields on that path. Especially not good enough to have his cattle looking as fat as they were. He tried to think of something else, but to no avail. So he reasoned that he just had to see what was going on.

The next day as the boy was getting ready to head out with the cattle. He looked at the old man and said jokingly, ‘I will be back soon. Do not follow me okay?’

The old man nodded dismissively in agreement but as soon as the boy left, he stood up and headed in his direction. He retraced the young boy's footsteps. His bare feet met the ground in graceful silence, ensuring every step he took was as silent as a stalking tiger. He soon caught up to the boy and became even stealthier.

The two walked on for a while, and the young boy was oblivious to his newfound company. They walked on and on until the boy suddenly stood still. He looked around to see if anyone was there.

The old man had already stashed himself behind an Acacia tree. He leaned closer to the tree trunk and breathed on an army of ants that were making their way up the tree. A few ants that met the old man's breath unexpectedly fell to the ground. The old man closed his eyes and waited.

When the young boy saw that there was no one with him, he raised his shepherd's stick in his right hand. The cattle looked at him expectantly, and the old man popped his head around the tree trunk to watch. The young boy continued to lift the stick even higher in the air and then, *thump,* he let the stick hit the ground next to him. A great heap of fresh green grass suddenly appeared in the now damp soil. The cows wasted no time and began to eat the grass.

'Huuuuh!' the old man gasped loudly for air. His eyes were wide with shock.

The young boy turned to see the old man looking at him with his jaw dropped.

The old man took a step back and stumbled on a rock. He immediately got back up and ran away in fear.

That day, the old man waited by the fire for the young boy, but the boy never returned. Then, when night came, the old man looked up at the sky and saw the Polaris star shining bright in the night sky.

Slim-Jan and Dom-Jan

Working in the Garden

Once upon a time, on a hot and sunny day, two friends marched the endless curves of a stony dirt road. They suffered the length of the road in hopes of getting a job they heard about earlier that day through village gossip. They heard that a Boer farmer was looking for two boys to help him with his garden work. So the friends packed up their clothes, took their sacks, and began to troop the endless road.

The two boys' names were Slim-Jan and Dom-Jan. Slim-Jan, who was tall and lean, was the smarter of the two. He hoped that this new journey would bring more excitement than the life he was leaving behind in the village. As they passed the rows of monotonous trees along the road, Slim-Jan was reminded of the ritualistic routine of chores he was leaving behind. His friend Dom-Jan had bulky muscles, but very little brain power. He was on the road for a much simpler reason. All he wanted was to work hard and do a good job.

And so, the two friends walked for miles under the burning sun. A few hours passed and the sun began to set under the African horizon. Just before the boys lost their eyes to the darkness, they saw the Boer's farm. The farmer, who had seen the boys approaching, headed over to greet them. He wore an old t-shirt with a rough pair of jean-shorts. His big potbelly reached the boys before the rest of his body followed.

'Ah, you boys must be here for the job. Welcome, welcome,' the Boer said as he shook their hands.

The boys nodded silently as they forced stale smiles on their faces.

'Come, let me show you to your room,' the farmer continued after reading their jaded expressions. 'We can talk about the work once you have both rested well.'

The boys followed the farmer into a small wooden cottage which had two beds in it. The Boer lit a candle and placed it in the middle of the two beds. The only other thing in the room was a worn-out armchair.

'All right, this will be your sleeping place. I will see you boys in the morning.'

The Boer walked out of the room and shut the door behind him. Tired from the long journey, the boys chose their beds and went to sleep.

The next morning Dom-Jan opened the door of their cottage to invite their new world in. The soil was a tinted brown colour, and the trees were bigger and greener than they were back home. Slim-Jan, who saw the Boer coming, came to join his friend at the door.

'Ah, nice to see that I didn't have to wake you boys up. Follow me, I will show you where you can get your breakfast. Once you are done, join me in the garden over there,' he said as he pointed to a big garden fenced off from the rest of the open fields.

The boys got two equally filling portions of food and ate their bellies full. When they finished their plates they headed over to the Boer who was now standing at the entrance to the garden.

The garden's dirt-brown soil was overgrown with small green weeds. The farmer instructed them to clear the garden of all the weeds so that it was ready in time for the sowing season.

'Leave that to us, we will have this garden ready for sowing in no time.' Slim-Jan said as he followed Dom-Jan into the garden to start working.

The boys started pulling out the weeds from the left corner of the garden, and the Boer stayed and watched them for a few more minutes.

Satisfied with what he saw the Boer said, 'Great work boys, carry on and I will come back in the late afternoon to see your progress.' He then left the boys to their work.

Once the Boer was out of sight, Slim-Jan stopped working. He looked around to find a tree that promised good shade from the now scorching hot sun. Right outside the garden's fence, he saw a big green Marula tree, whose shade was inviting him to take a nap. He left his friend Dom-Jan, who was still hard at work, and stretched his limbs out under the tree's shade. A row of ants that were marching down from the tree changed their flow to accommodate his limp body. A few minutes passed and Slim-Jan's snores started to fill the air.

After a few hours, the shadow of the Marula tree shrank and left Slim-Jan's feet out in the sun. The sun's sting on his feet woke him up. Slim-Jan stood up and stretched his limbs awake. He looked over to his friend Dom-Jan, who was still hard at work pulling out the weeds in the garden. Slim-Jan also saw how dirty Dom-Jan was. So he walked over to the garden hose and drenched himself. He then rolled around in the dirt. When he stood up he saw that he was now even dirtier than Dom-Jan. *Ah, perfect,* he thought.

Slim-Jan walked over to his friend and tardily began to pull the weeds out as well. Dom-Jan, who had grown up with his friend's lazy antics, was unfazed and simply continued working.

After a few minutes, the farmer made his way back to the garden. Slim-Jan saw him approaching and started working even harder. The Boer watched on in silence as he rubbed his big belly. He saw how much dirtier Slim-Jan was from all his hard work, and knew Slim-Jan did more work than Dom-Jan.

'Great, you boys can stop here today,' the Boer said. 'Go back to the kitchen and get something to eat. Slim-Jan, you should make sure to get the big plate of food for all your hard work.'

So the boys went to the kitchen to get their plates of food. Slim-Jan's plate was filled with a lot of porridge and big pieces of meat, while Dom-Jan's plate was much smaller. He only got a tiny piece of meat and a fist-sized portion of porridge. The boys sat down and ate their food before retreating to their room for the night.

The next few days went the same. The boys woke up, ate breakfast, and went to the garden.

Dom-Jan would immediately start working, while his friend Slim-Jan would sleep under the shade of his new favourite tree.

When the day was almost over Slim-Jan would wake, drench himself in water, roll around in the dirt, and join his friend before the Boer came to check on them. He always looked dirtier and sweatier than his friend.

The Boer farmer would see his favourite worker covered in the dirt of a hard day of work and say the same thing every time,

'Well done Slim-Jan, you should make sure to get the bigger plate of food.'

And Slim-Jan would nod and smile at the farmer. Every day Slim-Jan had a big plate of food to eat, while Dom-Jan's plate was much smaller. Then the boys would go to sleep and do it all again the next day.

One day, the boys finished their breakfast and headed to the garden. Slim-Jan went straight for the comfort of his tree. He laid down in the now familiar soil and almost immediately fell asleep. Dom-Jan went over to work, pulling out weeds and trying to clear as much of the garden as he could.

That day the Boer decided he wanted to watch his favorite worker. He put on his farmer's hat and walked over to the garden. As he got closer, he could see that one of the boys was fast asleep under a tree.

That Dom-Jan is really something else. No wonder Slim-Jan was always dirtier, he thought.

He walked over determined to wake Dom-Jan from his sleep to do his fair share of work. But, when he got closer, he saw that it was Slim-Jan sleeping under the tree. Confused, he decided to hide behind a tree and see what would happen next.

Soon the shade of the Marula tree exposed Slim-Jan's feet to the sun's sting. Slim-Jan woke up and continued to do what he always did. He walked over to the garden hose and soaked himself with the water. Then he laid down and rolled around in the dirt. He looked sweaty and dirty. *Perfect,* he thought, as he walked over to his friend.

The Boer now understood what was happening all these days. He quietly walked over to the boys, and as he got closer, he smiled at the boys as he always did. Slim-Jan, who didn't see him coming, tried to look busy and hard at work.

'Ah this looks great boys, you are almost done. You can end here today and head over to the kitchen for your food.'

Slim-Jan wondered why he did not ask him to get the big plate of food like he always did. *He must have forgotten,* he thought as they headed over to the kitchen.

In the kitchen, the boys sat down to eat. When the plates came, the biggest plate of food the boys had seen was given to Dom-Jan, while Slim-Jan got a small plate of porridge with no meat.

'Oh, hahaha, you confused us, I get the big plate of food,' Slim-Jan said as he moved to exchange the plates.

'No!' the Boer said as he walked over to the boys. 'Today I watched you very closely and I know what you both have been doing. There is no mistake here,' he said with so much disappointment.

Avoiding the farmer's gaze, Slim-Jan shamefully sat back down and ate his food quietly.

The Boy's Pact

Summer was coming to an end, and Slim-Jan and Dom-Jan were now at home living with their mothers. This meant that the two boys had a long list of chores to do every day. They had to care for the animals, maintain the yard, collect the firewood, and do whatever other tasks their mothers ordered them to do.

One early morning, the boys were woken up and told to head into the forest to collect firewood. Slim-Jan was not happy about this. As the boys weaved through the forest trees looking for good firewood, Slim-Jan fussed on and on about all the chores they had to do for their mothers.

'How do they just expect us to do whatever they want, whenever they want? "Clean the yard Slim-Jan! Feed the chickens Slim-Jan! Fetch me some firewood Slim-Jan!"' he mocked his mother's stern voice.

Dom-Jan ignored his friend's all-too-familiar rant. He also was not excited about being up so early, but he did not bother complaining about it. Instead, he focused his energy on scanning the forest floor for good firewood. The wood had to be dark in colour, and dry enough to keep a fire going. So far, all Dom-Jan could see were little thin twigs used for starting fires. After a few more minutes of walking, he finally saw a good spread of wood. He walked over and started stacking them together.

Slim-Jan followed his friend and slowly helped him pile the wood into a stack.

'Dom-Jan,' Slim-Jan said as he put the last wood on the pile. 'I know what we should do! We should kill our mothers.'

Dom-Jan spun around to look at his friend.

'What do you mean "kill our mothers"?! Why would we do that?' Dom-Jan insisted.

'So that we can be free of their nagging and chores. Have you not been listening?!' Slim-Jan turned away from his friend, looking deep into the forest as he continued speaking, 'See, all we have to do is...'

And so, the two boys were up early the next morning, ready to carry out their plan. Under the bright moonlight, Slim-Jan and Dom-Jan each creeped over to their mother's huts.

Dom-Jan entered his mother's hut and saw her sleeping on a thin mat in the centre of the hut. He quietly leaned over and killed her. It was done! He sighed a breath of relief, thankful that she did not wake up to see his betrayal.

Meanwhile, in the other hut, Slim-Jan bowed his tall frame to fit through the door. Once inside, he found his mother sound asleep. Quiet. She looked so innocent. Slim-Jan started to feel sorry for his mother and did not want to kill her anymore. He bent over and gently nudged her awake.

'Wake up Mama.'

'What? What is it son?' she said, still delirious with sleep.

'I need to keep you safe from Dom-Jan.' He lied, 'I am afraid he wants to kill you.'

'Nonsense! Why would that boy want to kill me?'

'I don't know Mama, but let's not stay to find out. Come on, follow me!' he said as he stood her up and walked over to the door.

He listened closely for any noise from outside. Nothing. He then opened the door slightly and popped his head through.

'All right, it's safe we can go. Just stay close to me Mama!'

Slim-Jan held his mother's hand as they ran for the forest. They soon started threading through the forest trees, getting further and further away from their village. Slim-Jan knew that he had to find a place that Dom-Jan didn't know, or go to a safe place to hide his mother.

After a few minutes of running, he was satisfied that he had found a good spot. He let go of his mother's now sweaty hand. His mother, who was out of breath, plumped herself loudly on the ground.

'You will be safe here Mama. Try and rest while I start to dig.'

Slim-Jan got a big stick and began to dig a hole for his mother. The sun came up while Slim-Jan was hard at work. He dug and dug until the hole was deep enough for his mother to stand in. Then he lowered his mother into the hole and got some leaves and sticks to cover the hole.

'Perfect,' he said once he had finished. 'You will be safe in there Mama, and I will bring you food and water every day.'

'Okay my son.'

'When I come, I will whistle three times so that you know that it is me passing by. Only then do you speak, okay Mama?'

'Yes son, I will be waiting.'

Slim-Jan turned around and went back to their village.

When he got back to the village, Dom-Jan was already there waiting for him.

'Why did it take you so long,' he asked.

'My mother is much fatter than yours Dom-Jan. It took me a lot more time to carry her and to dig a grave big enough for her,' Slim-Jan joked. 'But now we are finally free!'

'Yes, we are,' Dom-Jan agreed.

So the two boys started to live on their own. Finally freed from their mothers, they worked, cooked, and joked, all in their own time.

At midday, Slim-Jan took a plate of leftover food and some water, and headed out into the forest. He retraced his footsteps, and soon found himself close to where he hid his mother. Then he whistled three times.

'Yes, my son I am over here,' his mother called out.

Slim-Jan walked over and uncovered the hole. He lowered the food and water for his mother, who thanked him and started to eat the food.

Then he covered up the hole and headed back to the village. When he got to the village, Dom-Jan was seated outside his hut watching him intently.

'Where did you go Slim-Jan?'

'Oh, I just decided to take a walk. Don't you worry about me my friend.'

Later that day, the friends cooked, laughed, and did everything as they willed. Weeks went by with the same routine. Every day at midday, Slim-Jan took the leftover food and some water to his mother. His friend Dom-Jan watched him curiously as he headed out, and came back every day from his walks. Even though Dom-Jan wished to accompany him, Slim-Jan always refused. He said that he needed some time alone to think, something that Dom-Jan could not do.

Dom-Jan always wondered what Slim-Jan got up to in the middle of the woods.

One day, his curiosity got the best of him, and he decided to follow his friend. He sat by his hut and waited for Slim-Jan to head for the forest. Then he got up and followed his friend through the forest. As he walked under the hot afternoon sun, he realised that his friend was taking a path they had never taken before. *Why is he taking this route? What is he up to?* he thought.

Then after a few minutes of walking, his friend stopped and whistled three times.

'I am over here my son,' Slim-Jan's mother said.

Dom-Jan soon realised what was happening. He watched with anger as his friend uncovered the hole, and gave his mother the food and water. Afraid that his friend might see him, Dom-Jan ran back home. When he got back to the village he sat where he always sat as he waited for his friend. *He wanted us to do it? Why would he still keep her alive after I killed my mother?* he thought as he sat there alone.

A few minutes later, Slim-Jan came marching home. He greeted his friend with a warm smile.

'Good day Dom-Jan,' he said, 'is it not such a beautiful day my friend?'

'Where do you go every day?' Dom-Jan asked hiding his anger from his friend.

'Oh just walking about, don't mind me.'

Very early the next morning, while Slim-Jan was still asleep, Dom-Jan headed back into the forest. He followed the path he remembered his friend taking. Then when he got close to where he thought the hole was, he whistled three times.

'I am over here son, you are quite early today.'

Dom-Jan followed the voice. He uncovered the hole and immediately killed Slim-Jan's mother. 'It is only fair,' he said when it was all done. Then he covered the hole again and went back to the village.

When he got back to the village, Slim-Jan was not yet awake, so Dom-Jan snuck back into his hut and pretended to be asleep. When the boys woke up, the day went on as normal. Then when afternoon came, Slim-Jan secretly packed some food and some water, and headed for the forest. Dom-Jan saw his friend leaving and asked him like he did every day,

'Where are you going Slim-Jan?'

'Oh don't worry about it. I am just going for a walk.'

Slim-Jan followed the path that had become all too familiar for him. He was soon at his mother's hole and he whistled three times. He heard nothing back. He whistled another three times. Still, nothing. Slim-Jan searched for the hole, and when he found it, he quickly uncovered it. He saw his mother's lifeless body curled up at the bottom of the hole. Slim-Jan cried out loud in horror.

Evening came and Slim-Jan finally made his way back to the village. When he got there, he saw his friend was seated by the fire, and so he joined him.

He sat in silence and could not help but let a few tears roll down his face.

'Slim-Jan, why are you crying?'

'Oh it's nothing. It is just the smoke from the fire getting into my eyes.'

Dom-Jan watched his friend some more before asking again.

'Slim-Jan, why are you crying?'

'I told you Dom-Jan. The smoke keeps coming into my eyes, that's all.'

'Is it the smoke? Are you sure that it is not because I killed your mother today?'

Kazandona and the Giant

Once upon a time, in the green African rainforest, there lived a young boy named Kazandona. Like all young boys his age, Kazandona loved adventure. He would often go out alone on long walks through the forest, playing games as he went along.

One day Kazandona went out for another one of his walks. Boyishly wandering through the dense forest, Kazandona leapt onto a tree branch that had fallen to the ground and balanced his way across its length. Today, the forest was alive with wonder, and Kazandona's mind found amusement in everything. He listened to the birds singing in their nest, climbed some trees to test his strength, and soon started following an army of ants as they marched along the dark brown forest soil.

Kazandona watched intently as the single stream of ants climbed over the twigs and dried leaves that littered the forest floor. He walked alongside the ants, making sure not to step on his new friends. Then suddenly Kazandona bumped into something big and hard. He knew it was not a tree but something living, as he could now hear it breathing.

He slowly looked up to see what it was.

Kazandona jumped back. It was a giant cannibal.

The giant was tall and black, with broad shoulders, and big muscly arms that reached to the ground. All he had on was a pair of black shorts that ended right above his big knees. The giant was bare-chested, barefooted, and looking right back at Kazandona with a sinister grin on his face.

Gulp. 'Sorry mister. I was just on my way home. I did not mean to bump into you.'

'Little boy, little boy. Don't you know the forest is no playground? It is a shame that you will not live to learn this lesson,' the giant said as he reached out to grab Kazandona.

Kazandona was a smart boy, and he also knew that the giants were not the smartest of people. So before the giant's hand reached him, he screamed out,

'WAIT!!!'

The giant stopped and looked at his meal with a raised eyebrow.

'What is it child?'

'You should not eat me, because... because.... because I have magical powers.'

'Magical powers?' the giant scoffed. 'You will have to prove these so-called powers.'

'Oh but of course! Haha, no problem. But if I show you my powers, you cannot eat me. Otherwise I will have to use my powers on you.'

'Hurry up before I get bored!'

Kazandona looked around for anything he could use. The forest around him proved useless. So he stuck his hands in his pockets and retrieved everything inside. Some candy, small rocks, a candle stick, and a box of matches. *This will have to do,* he thought.

'Are you ready? Look around us. Do you see any water?'

He paused to give the giant some time to scan the forest around them. After he had looked around, the giant shook his head in response.

'Well, what if I told you I could make water appear using only this candle stick and a box of matches?' Kazandona continued.

'Impossible,' the giant protested excitedly.

'Watch this.'

Kazandona put the rest of his stuff back in his pocket and held out the candle for the giant to see. He then lit a matchstick and used it to light the candle. The candle started burning. Slowly the candle wax started melting down the side of the candle. He brought the candle closer to the giant for him to see the clear liquid falling down the sides of the candle.

'DO YOU SEE IT?! IT'S WATER!' he shouted. 'Water from a candle, using nothing but fire.'

Kazandona waited nervously to see if his trick worked.

Gasp. 'Yes I see the water. Wow, that is some real magic,' the giant said wide-eyed.

Kazandona quickly blew the candle out and put it back in his pocket.

'I'm glad you see my power. You are safe from me today. I will not use my magic on you, but I cannot promise for tomorrow.'

Not trying to push his luck, Kazandona immediately turned around and headed home.

'Have a good day little magician,' the giant called after him.

Kazandona raised his hand theatrically in response, not stopping to turn around as he did.

The Jackal and the Hyena

The Boer's Farm

A long time ago, in the tall straw grass of the African Savanna, lived two best friends: a Jackal and a Hyena. The two unlikely friends teamed up out of necessity. Not dominating the food chain, they quickly realised that there was strength in numbers. The Jackal would come up with plans for them to catch food, and the Hyena would mindlessly carry out the instructions shouted at him.

It was now winter in the Savanna. The leaves on the trees that had not already fallen off were now dried to a bright yellow colour. The Jackal and the Hyena laid belly-flat under one such Baobab tree.

The friends were not happy that it was winter, because the food they were usually catching followed the summer's sun north. Now the Jackal and the Hyena were left hungry.

'How much longer can we go without food?' the Hyena mumbled, making no effort to lift his head as he did.

'Not much longer,' the Jackal quietly responded.

He turned to lie on his side as he continued to watch the swarm of flies that circled the Hyena's snout. As their buzzing sound filled the air, he was thankful that they were drawn to the Hyena and not him. After a while, he let other thoughts crowd his mind.

Hours passed as the two friends lay under their Baobab tree in mindless hunger, constantly tossing and moaning.

Then suddenly, the Jackal lit up with excitement.

'I got it!' He yelled as he sprang to his paws. 'We can eat the sheep at the farm.'

The Hyena made no effort to respond. All the animals knew not to eat the sheep of the angry farmer. No, no, no! The angry farmer had a whip which never missed and always wailed louder than its victims. But the Jackal continued, ignoring his friend's disinterest.

'I have a plan you see. We will go during the night and...' the Jackal continued explaining his plan.

The Hyena lifted his head and started to grin as the Jackal continued to explain. *Finally, a promise of food,* he thought to himself as he let out a faint laugh.

When night finally came, it found the two friends already on the road to the farm. The two walked on in the long grass as the stars lit their way. Soon, they came to the clear field that marked the beginning of the farm. The two friends stepped out of the long straws of grass and walked through the open field of cut grass. They headed straight for the enclosure that housed the sheep, being as quiet and as stealthy as they could.

When they finally reached the fence, the Jackal turned to his friend and whispered,

'Okay, now dig very quietly.'

The Hyena let out a slight laugh before digging his claws into the reddish-brown soil under the fence. The Jackal rolled his eyes at his mindless companion before looking over their surroundings to see if they had woken anything up. The sheep lay sound asleep inside the enclosure, unaware of the trouble that was busy digging its way in. The farmer's house that stood alone in the darkness was quiet as well. *It was safe,* the Jackal thought to himself.

Soon, the Hyena's mindless pursuit had the two friends in the enclosure. The Hyena pounced on the first sheep his paws could touch, and dug into his dinner. The Jackal, not wanting to make any more noise, slowly approached his first sheep, and dug in and ate.

The two friends were so hungry that they said nothing at all as they filled their empty tummies. The Hyena greedily stuffed his face, focusing only on the relief each bite gave him. Meanwhile, the Jackal ate his first sheep, and after he had finished, he went back to the hole under the fence. He then tried to squeeze himself through the hole. Satisfied that it was still big enough, he slowly approached his next sheep.

And so the two continued. After every sheep, the Jackal would check to see if he could fit through the hole. When he couldn't, he dug the hole a bit deeper for himself, but the Hyena only focused on eating as much as he could. By the time the Jackal was on his third sheep, the Hyena had already eaten six sheep, and his belly was getting big and round.

After a while, the Hyena's careless frenzy woke all the sheep up, and the sheep began to cry out for their master.

'Mm-m-mmaster, mm-m-mmaster,' they cried loud into the quiet darkness. 'Mm-m-mmaster, mm-m-mmaster.'

The farmer was a diligent man. Having lived many years in the unforgiving African Savanna, he knew all too well the importance of protecting what he had. His perceptive ears never slept, and soon a light went on in the farmhouse.

The door swung open and the angry man appeared bare-chested through the door, holding the infamous whip. The Jackal, who was surveying his surroundings every now and then, saw him first. His white potbelly reflected the night's stars as he stomped over to his sheep.

The Jackal got up and ran to the fence. He shot himself through the hole, which was just big enough for him, and made it to the other side.

Startled by his friend, the Hyena got up to see what had happened. Had he been a smarter animal, he would have known to follow his friend right away. But he was not.

He slowly scanned the night's darkness until he finally saw him. The angry farmer was standing a few steps behind him.

The first lash swished onto the Hyena's back before he even moved to the hole.

He cried out after his friend, but the night's darkness had already swallowed the Jackal. *Swish,* came the second whip, and the Hyena dashed to the fence. He dove into the hole and tried to wiggle his way out, but he was stuck. His round belly was too big and got caught on the fence above him. He could not crawl out.

The farmer followed after him to the hole, and let the whip land two more times on the helpless Hyena. The Hyena cried out with every whip, still trying to wiggle himself out. Then the farmer raised his hand high in the air and let the third whip land heavily on the Hyena's bum. The Hyena jerked forward so sharply from the pain that he finally freed himself.

Ignoring the sharp pain that was still pounding from his back and bum, the Hyena let his legs carry him into the darkness as fast as they could.

The Jackal's Great Trick

Summer had come again to the Savanna planes and the two friends, the Jackal and the Hyena, were lying under their favourite Baobab tree. They stayed under the tree's shadow to hide from the harsh burn of the summer's sun. Just outside the shadow of their tree, the sun's heat could be seen slowly weaving into the reddish-brown soil. Although they were hungry, the friends decided to wait for the cool night's air to hunt for food.

The Hyena filled the time waiting by retelling the stories of the past adventures the two friends had lived through.

'Remember... remember that time, when we were lost in the desert?' he asked.

The Jackal ignored the cackles of his friend and kept his mind busy by studying his view instead. From their tree, he could see all the animals of the Savanna playing the game of life.

Right in front of them, the elephants crowded around the only watering hole. They were trying to keep cool by splashing themselves with the mud-brown water. In the yellow grass behind them, the zebras were eating their lunch with pointed ears, listening closely for the sounds of danger.

And further away, under a tree just like theirs, a pride of lions were grooming each other. One lioness haughtily stalked about, keeping watch over her little cubs that were wrestling each other.

Back under their tree, the Hyena continued droning on about their silly stories, not realizing that his friend had long stopped listening.

A few hours passed and the Jackal suddenly saw something moving in the grass. What was it? Was it, one of the zebras? No, it was a sheep. All alone? He couldn't believe his eyes. The African Savanna was an unforgiving home, and dinner never served itself. But today, the Savanna gave him a gift, he thought. He could not share this rare gift.

The Jackal quietly scanned the horizon for anything he could use to rid himself of his friend. Then he saw it.

He sprang to his feet and went dashing through the grass. The Hyena, who was left mid-way into his tenth story of the day, watched his friend with confusion. He then jumped up and followed after him.

The Jackal ran through the straws of grass before making his way up a steep hill. He dodged a few anthills as he ran up the hill. Then, out of breath and finally at the top, he saw the big stone that he had seen from the shade of their tree. He put his paws on its rough surface and pushed all his weight against the big stone.

The Hyena, who had been chasing after his friend, finally caught up with him. He was out of breath and disappointed that the Jackal's teeth were not sunk into an early dinner.

'Wha... what is this? Why did you... have us run up this hill for a stone?' He asked still panting for breath.

'Did you not see it?' the Jackal asked, still pushing up against the boulder. 'It was rolling down the hill, headed straight for our favourite tree. Don't just stand there, HELP ME!' he demanded.

The Hyena immediately went to the stone and tried his best to stop the stone from rolling down the hill.

'How long can we hold it up Jackal?'

'Not very long, not on our own at least. But if we both leave, it's going to roll right over our favorite tree. You don't want that, do you?'

The Hyena shook his head in response and the Jackal knew to continue.

'Well, you are the strongest out of the two of us. I am sure you can hold it steady while I go and get the other animals to help us.'

'You are right, I am pretty strong. But hurry back. I don't know how long I can hold it.'

The Jackal slowly backed away from the stone with his hands still raised, as if he was ready to lean back on the stone if it rolled back even an inch. Satisfied that it didn't, he turned around and ran down the hill just as fast as he had come up.

'Hurry up,' the Hyena screamed after him.

The Jackal ran straight to the sheep. He had a wide smile on his face. He knew that his friend was dim, but he still loved to see a good effort at fooling him work out. He caught his sheep easily and started to fill his belly greedily.

An hour went by, and the Hyena now had sweat trailing down his strained face. *Where is the Jackal?* he thought. *Why is it taking him so long?*

The Hyena stopped. His thoughts were interrupted by a troop of five monkeys who were now noisily jumping and playing on the stone.

'Hey, hey, hey. Get off the stone!' the Hyena immediately demanded. 'Can you not see that I am trying to hold up this big stone! It is already heavy, and you guys jumping on it is not helping!'

'Ooo ooo aaahaahaha.' The monkeys laughed hysterically.

'What is so funny?! Get off!'

'Ooo ooo aaa aaa. Why are you holding up a stone that stands perfectly on its own? Ooo ooo...'

'I don't have time for your games.' The Hyena snapped, 'My friend saw this stone rolling down, and heading straight for our tree. So just get off!'

'Aaahaahaha, ooo ooo aaahaahaha.' The monkeys laughed even more, rolling all around the stone and rubbing their bellies as they did.

The biggest monkey in the troop saw how serious the Hyena was. He stopped laughing and said,

'I have played on this stone for years and years. Before that, my fathers and their father before them played on it. For thousands of years, this rock stood, and it has never rolled off this hill. Leave the stone and see for yourself.'

'I will not leave the...'

'JUST LEAVE IT!' all the monkeys shouted back.

The Hyena reluctantly left the stone, his arms raised forward in front of him, ready to spring back on the stone if he saw even the slightest movement.

Nothing.

'See, we told you so. Ooo oooo aaaa aaaa,' the big monkey said before they all went back to playing their game.

The Hyena, worn from holding the stone, walked down the hill in confusion. He didn't understand why the Jackal thought the stone was going to roll down.

Then, as he reached the bottom of the hill, he saw his friend in the distant grass. He was nibbling at the meat left in between a cleanly eaten rib. The Hyena understood now what had happened. He ran angrily to his friend screaming,

'You selfish...!'

Snonnapo

A long, long time ago, in a big and busy village, there lived a young girl named Snonnapo. Snonnapo lived in a hut with her mum and dad, and a little white fluffy dog. Snonnapo's parents loved their daughter dearly, but they were not the only ones. She was adored by her whole village because she was the kindest and the prettiest girl in the village. She had beautiful black skin that glistened under the sun's rays, and short brown hair that she kept braided in small twists. Snonnapo greeted everyone with a warm smile, and always made time to lend a helping hand.

The village people never grew tired of singing her praises.

'Have you seen that beautiful Snonnapo today?' they would ask.

'Yes, she was helping old Mama by the river. She truly has the heart of an angel.'

'What a beauty she is.'

'The most beautiful,' they all agreed.

Snonnapo had three best friends. When she was not doing her chores, she would spend her time playing games with her friends in the forest. The four girls would play, laugh, and joke until the sun set. Then they would each go home to sleep.

Snonnapo's friends enjoyed playing with her too, but they were also jealous of her. Every day, they would hear all the compliments Snonnapo received, and always wished that they were as loved or as beautiful as her.

One day, the friends grew tired of Snonnapo's perfection and they decided to kill her.

The three friends went over to Snonnapo's house. They saw her mother sitting under the shade of her hut and walked over to her, smiling as widely as they could.

'Good afternoon Ma,' the children said all together.

'Good afternoon little ones.'

'Ma, we want to go play with Snonnapo. Can she come and play with us?' the tallest of the friends asked shyly.

'I don't know girls. You will have to ask her father.'

'Okay Ma.'

The children looked around to see where he was.

'Look! There he is,' one of the girls said as she pointed to Snonnapo's dad.

He was seated under the shade of a big tree with the family dog. The girls quietly walked over to him.

'Good afternoon Uncle,' they sang.

'Good afternoon my children.'

'Uncle, can Snonnapo come and play with us today?' one of the girls asked politely.

'I don't know children. You will have to ask her mother.'

'We did Uncle, but she told us to ask you.'

'Ah okay,' Snonnapo's father said scratching his head. 'Yes, it's fine. You can take Snonnapo and go play.'

'Thank you Uncle!'

The girls rushed over to Snonnapo, who was watching them from inside the hut.

'Come Snonnapo, let's go play!'

And so the girls went off running, skipping and laughing into the forest. Snonnapo's little dog followed closely behind the girls as they went deeper into the forest. Soon, they came to the clearing where they always played their games. This time, there was a deep hole, right next to the clearing on the far east side. Snonnapo's friends came earlier that day to dig up the hole, and placed burning firewood at the bottom of the hole.

The friends immediately started playing a game of touch tag, and Snonnapo was having so much fun she did not even notice the new hole next to their playing field.

The girls continued to chase each other a round and a round. One of the girls started chasing Snonnapo. Snonnapo laughed and ran faster as she tried to get away from her friend. She did not notice that she was headed straight for the big hole. As she was running, she looked behind to see how far her friend was.

'Hahahaha, you can't catch...'

Whoosh!

She fell into the pit.

Her friends waited by the edges of the pit for fire to burn their friend. After a long while, Snonnapo was gone, but her bones were still there.

'These bones are never going to burn away, what should we do?' one of the friends asked.

The girls sat in silence as they tried to think of a solution. One of the girls saw the little fluffy dog also seated next to them by the pit and said,

'I know what we can do! We can give her bones to her dog.'

'Ah, that's a great Idea.'

The girls pulled some of the bones from the pit and tried to feed them to the dog.

'Here you go little doggy. Here doggy, doggy,' one of the girls said as she offered a bone to the dog.

The tearful dog refused the bone and started to sing in a sad whisper:

♫ They killed Snonnapo,

And gave me the bones of Snonnapo.

But I wouldn't eat Snonnapo,

When it's my owner Snonnapo.

Snonnapo, Snonnapo...

Snonnapo, Snonnapo. ♫

The girls looked over at the dog.

'What is this mutt saying,' one girl asked.

'I don't know, I can't understand it. Just feed it the bones already.'

The girls tried again to feed the dog the bone, but the dog just started singing again:

♫ They killed Snonnapo,

And gave me the bones of Snonnapo.

But I wouldn't eat Snonnapo,

When it's my owner Snonnapo.

Snonnapo, Snonnapo...

Snonnapo, Snonnapo. ♫

The girls still did not understand the little dog.

'Agg, let's just bury the bones and be done with this. I'm tired of this little dog.'

So the girls buried Snonnapo's bones in the hole and headed back home.

That night, the little dog went back home. He found Snonnapo's parents seated around the evening fire. The little dog sat himself softly by the father's feet.

'Where is Snonnapo?' Snonnapo's mother asked her husband.

'I don't know, she is usually back by now. Let us wait. I am sure she will be back soon,' he answered as he stared into the distance in search of his little girl.

Into the night's silence, the little dog started singing again.

♫ They killed Snonnapo,

And gave me the bones of Snonnapo.

But I wouldn't eat Snonnapo,

When it's my owner Snonnapo.

Snonnapo, Snonnapo...

Snonnapo, Snonnapo. ♫

The mother looked at the dog in shock.

'Did you hear what the dog said?'

'No, I did not. Sing again little doggy. What did you say?'

The little fluff sang again, with more sadness than the last time.

♫ They killed Snonnapo,

And gave me the bones of Snonnapo.

But I wouldn't eat Snonnapo,

When it's my owner Snonnapo.

Snonnapo, Snonnapo...

Snonnapo, Snonnapo. ♫

The parents gasped for air as they realised what their dog was telling them.

Journey to a Wife

Once upon a time, there lived a father and his two sons. The family lived on a very big farm with green open fields.

On their farm, they grew fresh fruits and vegetables and had plenty of cows and chickens. They had everything they could ever ask for. Well, almost everything.

There was one thing their big farm did not have, and that was wives for the sons to marry. The eldest son was the most eager to find a wife.

One night, the family was seated around the fire, each deep in their thoughts. The father and the youngest son were quietly staring at the small sparks floating away from the fire's flame. The eldest son watched their focus with mocking interest. *Ah, how fascinating, a fire*, he thought.

'Pa, I need a wife,' the eldest son finally broke the silence.

'Yes son, you do. You are getting very old,' his father said matter-of-factly.

'Well, you are not going to find her seated here with us,' the younger brother chimed in.

'Ah, wisdom has found you yet little brother. Yes, I will have to go and find her. I can leave tomorrow morning if Father allows?'

'Yes, yes. Go before your hair is as white as sheep's wool.'

And so, early the next morning, the eldest son packed some fruits and water into his leather satchel. When he was ready, he waved goodbye to his family and headed for the road.

With his head held high and his chest out, he strode along the road. *I will walk to the next farm and ask for a wife there*, he thought.

The eldest son walked at a steady pace, neither fast nor slow. 'The fastest way to finish a long journey is to pace yourself,' he remembered his father's teaching.

Bored with the mundane task of walking, his mind drifted to thoughts of his future wife. He tried to imagine her beautiful face. 'I can't wait to meet her,' he thought aloud.

'Hey sir! Hey, could you please help us?' a tiny voice interrupted his day-dream.

The voice came from a row of ants that were on the ground next to him. The son looked dismissively at the tiny ants.

'What do you want from me?'

'We are trying to finish building our anthill,' one of the ants said, 'and we could use your help collecting some sand and bringing it closer to our hill, so we can build faster.'

The eldest son saw the half-built anthill and thought, *what an eyesore.* He walked over to the anthill and kicked it all down.

'I don't help tiny little ants!' He demanded once the anthill was levelled.

'You did not help us!' One of the ants said, frantically wagging its finger. 'We will remember this. Wherever you go, we will not be there for you, and we will not help you.'

The son waved them off as he continued walking.

'Psssh, what help do I need from a bunch of tiny little ants anyway.'

And so the son continued his journey. He had been walking all morning, and now the sun was shining bright in the sky. It was getting very hot, and he started to sweat. *It's not too far away now,* he thought as he continued to march under the harsh sun.

Then, in the forest next to him, he saw a duck lying under the shade of a big Baobab tree. The duck wanted to get to the lake, but the ground was too hot for his bare feet to bear.

'Help me, please dear boy. Help me!' The duck shouted over to the son when it saw him.

'Huh, what a needy forest,' the son said to himself as he walked over to it. 'What is it?! What do you need?'

'I need your help getting to the lake please,' the sweet voice of the duck said, 'it is too hot and my little feet cannot get me there fast enough. Could you please carry me to the lake?'

'Carry you to the lake?!' the boy scoffed at the request.

He came closer to the duck and kicked some dirt into its face.

'That's for wasting my time!' the son said before stomping away.

'You did not help me! *Cough-cough*.' The duck yelled after him, 'and I will remember this. *Cough*. Wherever you go, I will not be there with you, and I will not help you.'

'Try helping yourself first,' the son chuckled as he walked further down the road.

After a little while, he reached the lake that the duck was talking about. The air was cooler and carried with it a refreshing wind. The son looked at the patches of mint-green grass that grew next to the lake's still glittering waters. *Good thing that duck is not here to disturb this peace*, he thought to himself before he continued with his journey.

He walked on and on down the narrow path the forest provided. A few miles later, he heard another voice calling out to him.

'Help us... ppp-please help us,' a swarm of wasps said.

The wasps were buzzing around their nest that lay on the ground.

'Our nest fell to the ground, and we could use your help picking it back up and placing it on this tree branch,' one of the wasps asked kindly.

The eldest son was fed up with the constant calls for help. He kicked their nest as hard as he could manage.

'Stop asking me for help! I am busy with my own journey!' he demanded.

'YOU KICKED OUR NEST! We will remember this. Wherever you go, we will not be there with you, and we will not help you.'

'Huh, you seem pretty helpless anyway,' the son said before turning back to the road and continuing his journey.

He knew that the farm was only a little further down the road. Just as the sun began to set, he finally reached the farm.

The farmer, a dark and hairy man, came to the gate to greet him.

'Hello my boy, what are you doing here so late?'

'Hi Uncle, I am the son of the farmer just down this road. I have walked all the way here in search of a wife to marry. I know you have a daughter, and I would like her hand in marriage.'

'What a brave boy. Yes, my daughter needs to marry a brave and kind man. I will have to test you to see if you are worthy of my daughter.'

'Oh I am definitely worthy,' the son said, flexing his muscles for the farther to see.

'Yes well, come on in then. Today you can sleep and rest. We will do the tests tomorrow. If you pass my three tests, you can have my daughter's hand in marriage.'

And so, the farmer showed the son to a hut where he could rest for the night. When he was left alone, the son stretched his limbs out on a straw mat that was in the middle of the hut and fell asleep peacefully. He was not worried about the tests he had waiting for him in the morning. No, he was sure that he would pass any test that the farmer had for him.

Morning came and the farmer woke the boy up for them to eat breakfast together. After they finished their breakfast, the farmer walked with the boy to a big open garden for the first test.

The garden was enormous. It had thousands of mealie (maize) plants that were now ready for harvest.

'Your first test is to harvest all of these mealies before the afternoon. I will come back in the afternoon to see how you have done,' said the farmer before leaving the son to work.

The eldest son was used to this type of farm work, but he had never harvested such a big field on his own. *Let me start from one corner of the field*, he thought to himself.

He began harvesting the mealies as fast as he could. He pulled the ears from the stalk of the plants and pilled them up in one of the big bags he was given. The son did not stop or take a break once, but before he knew it, it was already afternoon.

His heart began to race as he saw the farmer approaching. He had only finished one corner of the big garden. He hung his head in shame as the farmer greeted him.

'Good afternoon my boy,' the farmer said once he was close enough.

'Afternoon Uncle,' the son responded meekly.

'I see you did not pass this test,' the farmer continued as he peered over the garden still filled with mealies. 'Let us go to the second test. Maybe you will do better there.'

The farmer and the son walked over to a well that stood in the middle of a clearing. When they got there, the son looked down the opening of the well and saw nothing but darkness. Next to the well was an empty wooden bucket that had a rope tied to its handles.

The farmer reached into the pocket of his pants and pulled out a silver spoon.

'You see this spoon?' the farmer said as he presented the spoon in his hand to the son. When he saw the son nod, he continued with his instructions. 'I want you to get this spoon from the bottom of the well. You have until the end of the day to retrieve it.'

The farmer then dropped the spoon into the well and left the son to his work.

The eldest son had a puzzled look on his face. He was wondering how he would get the spoon from the bottom of the well. He held on to the side of the well and stretched his hand in as far as he could, but the well was too deep. He could not even reach the water.

So the son crawled down to the bottom of the well. The well was filled with water. The son dove deep into the water and tried to feel for the spoon, but he could not hold his breath long enough to find the spoon at the bottom of the water. He tried over and over again, but to no avail. The spoon was too far down in the water.

Soon, the sun outside the well began to set. After a few minutes, the son saw the farmer's face covering the opening of the well.

'It's time for you to come up son,' the farmer said.

The son crawled up the well with nothing in his hands.

'You are empty-handed,' the farmer said once the son emerged from the hole.

'Yes Uncle, I tried my best.'

The farmer looked at the son who was drenched from the water in the well.

'Okay, you have one last test. Follow me.'

The son followed the farmer quietly. They walked back to a hut that was next to the farmer's hut. The farmer knocked on the hut before opening the door. Inside, there were three brides seated on the floor that were covered with a thick veil.

'For your last test, I want you to choose your wife. One of these three brides is my beautiful daughter. If you choose her, you can have her hand in marriage, but be careful not to choose the other two brides,' the farmer warned. 'One of them is a very ugly woman, and if you choose her, you will have to marry her and stay with her for the rest of your life. The other is a monster, a very dangerous beast. If you choose the beast, it will eat you whole.'

The son took a step back in the hut. Under the thick veil, all of the brides looked alike. He took a deep breath and pointed to the bride who sat in the middle.

'I choose her,' he said.

The bride stood up, and as she stood, her veil fell to the ground. The eldest son looked on as a big, hairy beast revealed itself. Before the son could scream or run, the beast swallowed him whole.

★ ★ ★

A year went by, and back at the farm, the youngest son also grew eager to find a wife. One night, as he sat around the fire with his father, he decided that it was time for him to go and find a wife.

'Father,' he said quietly.

'Yes, my son?'

'I think it is time for me to also go out there and find a wife.'

'No, no my son. It is too dangerous out there. It has been a year already and we still have not heard from your brother.'

'I know father, but I am becoming a man now. I need to do this. Please let me go and find my wife, and maybe I will also find my brother along the road.'

'Huh, okay my son. You can leave in the morning. But please be careful.'

'Thank you, Father. I will be very careful,' the son said with a big smile on his face.

When morning came, the son was wide awake and ready for his adventure. He took his leather satchel and packed some water and a few apples for the road. Then he walked over to his father who watched him uneasily.

'I will be careful father, I promise.'

'Go before it gets dark,' his father said waving him off to the road.

And so, the youngest son headed for the same road his brother took just a year ago. Although he was sad to leave his father behind, he knew that he had to do this.

As he walked along the road, he started to think about his future wife. *She has to be a good-hearted woman with whom I can raise my children,* he thought to himself. He thought about her character and values, and hoped he would be good enough for her.

'Hallow young man! Hi, please could you help us?' a tiny voice said, pulling the son's mind back to reality.

The son looked to the ground and saw that the voice came from an ant. A little further behind, the son could see rows of ants that were all busy rebuilding their anthill.

'Oh hi, how can I help you?'

'We are trying to build our home in time for the rainy reason. Could you please help us by collecting some sand and bringing it closer to our hill so we can build faster?'

'Yes, of course I will help you.'

'Thank you so much young man.'

And so, the youngest son walked over to the sandiest part of the forest. He piled up as much sand as he could in his hands and carried it over to the anthill. He did this again and again until the sand pile next to the anthill was up to his knees.

'Oh that is plenty enough,' one ant said as the son placed the last round of sand on the pile. 'You are so kind to have helped us! Thank you so much,' the ant continued. 'We will always remember this. Wherever you go, we will be there with you, and if you need help, we will help you just like you helped us.'

'It was my pleasure. Good luck building the rest of your home,' the son said as he returned to the road and continued his journey.

The sun was already high in the sky, but the young man did not mind. He enjoyed helping the little ants. He walked on and on under the heat of the sun, singing his favourite tune to himself.

His melody filled the air, and soon the duck heard him singing. The duck was hiding from the burning sun under the shade of another Baobab tree. Just like last year, it wanted to get to the lake, but could not bear to walk on the screeching hot ground.

When the son got closer, the duck called after him.

'Hello! Hello! Hi, can you please help me?'

The boy walked over to the duck and squatted down to talk to it.

'Hi little duck. How can I help you?'

'Oh, I just need help getting to the lake that's down the road. The ground is too hot for me to walk on with my bare feet. Could you please carry me to the lake?'

'Of course little duck. I am headed in that direction anyway,' the youngest son said as he stretched his hands out to the duck.

He gently picked the duck up and carried it in his arms to the lake. When he got to the lake, he kneeled as close to the water as he could. The duck climbed out of the son's arms and walked over to the cool lake water.

Then *whoosh,* the little duck jumped right into the sparkling water. It was so happy that it began to swim around in circles.

'Hahaha. How refreshing,' it said.

Finally, it looked over to the son who was now standing next to the lake watching.

'You helped me! Thank you so much, I will always remember this,' the duck said. 'Wherever you go, I will be there with you, and if you need help, I will help you just like you helped me.'

'It was my pleasure. Enjoy the water.'

He turned around and headed back to the road. *Not too much further now,* he thought to himself.

The sun was now shining softly in the sky, still lighting the way as the son trooped down the road. Not wanting to be alone in the forest after dusk, he began to walk a little faster. Just as his heels were picking up speed, he heard a buzzing voice call out for him.

'Help us... help us ppp-please!' a wasp said.

Right next to the road, the son saw a wasp's nest on the ground, and a swarm of wasps buzzing around it.

'Oh no. What happened?' the son asked as he pointed to the nest.

'Our nest fell to the ground again. Could you please help us put our nest back on the tree branch?' one of the wasps asked.

'Yes, of course I will help you.'

He carefully lifted the wasps' nest and walked over to a tree that the wasps led him to. Then he placed the nest on the tree branch and made sure it was secure.

'There we go. It should not fall from here anymore.'

'You helped us pick our nest back up! Thank you so much, we will always remember this,' one of the wasps said. 'Wherever you go, we will be there with you, and if you need our help, we will help you just like you helped us.'

'It was my pleasure. Goodbye,' the son said as he continued with his journey.

The sun had already set when the youngest son finally arrived at the farm. The farmer did not see him approaching, but he saw the farmer sitting by the fire.

'Hello Uncle,' he called out politely. 'Hi, please may I come to you.'

'Oh, yes young man, come over here.' The old man waited until the son was close enough before he continued, 'I did not see you through this darkness. What do you want my boy?'

'Hi Uncle. Sorry for coming so late. I am the youngest son of the farmer who lives down the road from you. I came here because I would like to ask for your daughter's hand in marriage.'

'Another one. My daughter is attracting you all like flies. See young man, my daughter needs a brave and kind man, so I will have to test you to see if you are worthy to marry my daughter.'

'She is lucky to have such a loving father,' the son said. 'I hope to one day love my children the same.'

'Hhmm. Come. Let me show you to your room for tonight. Be sure to rest very well tonight, because tomorrow we will have the test.'

The farmer took him to a hut that he could sleep in. The youngest son was so tired from his busy day that he immediately fell asleep.

When morning came, the farmer found the son seated in front of the hut patiently waiting for him. The two men had breakfast together before the farmer showed the son to the big garden.

'Your first test for the day is to harvest all of the mealies in this garden. You have to be done by this afternoon. If you are not done by the time I come back, then it means that you have failed the test,' the farmer explained.

The youngest son nodded his understanding, and the farmer left him to his work.

This garden is too big, I cannot finish it alone, the son thought as he headed for the garden.

'We are here to help,' he heard a voice say from the ground.

When he looked down, he saw rows and rows of ants lined up next to him. They were all ready to help him harvest the mealies. The son was very happy to see them.

'We told you that wherever you went, we would be there with you, and that if you needed our help, we would help you just like you helped us.'

'Thank you, my friends.'

And so, the youngest son and the army of ants went into the garden and started harvesting the mealies. The ants worked together to bite off the ears from the stalk of the plants, and then piled them up in big bags at the centre of the garden. The son also worked with them, pulling the ears from the plants as fast as he could and placing them in the bags.

After a few hours, they had finished harvesting all the mealies in the big garden. The youngest son thanked his little helpers and waved them goodbye as they marched away. Then he walked over to the closest tree and took a nap under its cool shade.

When the farmer came, he saw that the son was asleep under the shade of the tree. *This boy is not serious. What type of a man sleeps when he has work to do?* he thought to himself as he walked over to the boy. As he got closer to the garden, he saw that it was empty and all the mealies were piled up in the centre of the garden. The youngest son woke up to the farmer towering over him with a bright smile on his face.

'How did you do that?' the farmer asked.

'It was not easy but I had a little help from some tiny friends,' the son replied.

'I don't see your friends, but congratulations. You are the first man to ever complete this task. My daughter might find a man good enough for her after all,' the farmer said still in disbelief. 'Now, come on, let us go to the second task.'

The two men walked over to the well. When they got there, the farmer reached into his pocket and pulled out a silver spoon.

'See this spoon,' he said as he lifted the spoon to the son's face. 'I want you to retrieve this spoon from the bottom of the well. You have until the end of the day. Please don't let me down.'

The farmer then dropped the spoon into the well and returned to his hut.

'This well looks very deep. How will I get to the bottom of the well?' he thought aloud.

'Maybe I can help,' the sweet voice of the duck said.

'Little duck, you came to help me?'

'Yes, I did. I told you that wherever you went, I would be there with you, and if you ever needed my help, I would help you just like you helped me.'

'Thank you little duck.' The son looked around and saw the wooden bucket on the side of the well. 'Can you fit in the bucket?' he asked the duck.

'I think so. Let me try.' The duck walked over and hopped into the bucket that was just big enough.

'Okay great, I will lower you down the well, then you can get the spoon,' the son said.

So the son lifted the bucket by the ropes that were tied to its handles. Then he lowered the bucket to the bottom of the well. When the bucket reached the water, the duck hopped out and dove deep into the water.

The duck was an expert swimmer and could hold his breath underwater for a long time. After a few minutes, the duck emerged from the water with seven spoons in his beak. He got back into the bucket and placed the spoons under its feet.

'Okay, lift me out of here,' he yelled up to the son.

The son pulled the bucket back out of the well.

'Thank you so much little duck,' the youngest son said as he collected the spoons from the bucket.

'My pleasure,' the duck said as it waddled away.

The son sat by the well and waited for the farmer. When the sun began to set, the farmer appeared from the forest trees. As he came closer, he saw the seven spoons in the son's hand.

'I was not sure which one was mine, so my friend and I got them all,' the son said as he held out the spoons for the farmer.

'Hahaha, these friends of yours are amazing. You passed the test.' The farmer took the spoons from the son's hands. 'It's a good thing you came along. I was starting to run out of spoons. Come, let us go to the last test.'

The farmer walked joyfully with the son to the last test. He had a feeling that his little girl had finally found her husband.

When they got to the hut that housed all the brides, the farmer knocked on the door before leading the son into the hut. The three wives were all seated on the ground with the same thick veil covering them.

'My son, for your last test, I want you to choose your wife. One of these three brides is my beautiful daughter. The other is a hideous woman, and the last is a monster. If you choose my daughter, you can have her hand in marriage. But be careful! If you choose the ugly maid, then you will have to marry and live with her forever. And if you choose the beast, then it will eat you where you stand.'

What difficult options, the son thought to himself. He tried his best to make out which of the three brides was a beast, but he could not see what was under the veils.

Then he heard a buzzing sound. A few wasps had entered the hut and hovered over the last woman. *'Wherever you go, we will be with you,'* he remembered the wasps saying, *'and if you need our help, we will help you just like you helped us.'*

With the confidence of a raging bull, he lifted his hand and pointed to the last girl.

'I choose her as my wife Uncle.'

The last bride stood up and let her veil fall from her head. As the veil hit the ground, the youngest son saw the most beautiful woman he had ever seen in his life.

The End

ACKNOWLEDGMENTS

First and foremost, I give thanks to my Creator, and the center of my life, King Jesus. Through His grace and favor, I found the creativity, strength, and endurance to write and publish this book. I am forever grateful for His presence and guidance in my life.

I am especially thankful to my talented friend, Ufuomaoghene Akpokiniovo, whose artistry truly brings these pages to life. Your creativity and dedication have been invaluable to this project.

To my parents, Steve Matjituavi Rukoro and Alma Tavizee Rukoro, a heartfelt thank you for your love, encouragement, and unwavering support in all that I do. You have been my foundation.

To my lovely sister and brother, Inomasa Rukoro and Mbeutjeka Rukoro, and my dear friend, Lorraine Phakamea, thank you for cheering me on, for believing in me, and for standing beside me every step of the way.

Lastly, to my family, the Rukoros, the Zamuees, the Katoores, the Ngutonuas, the Kenaihes, the Mbuendes, the Mapohas, and the Veiis; to my church family in RTN; and to my many friends, there are too many of you to name here, but please know that your love, encouragement, and kindness have carried me through. This book is as much yours as it is mine.